When Hope Calls

By David Lui

Dedicated to the countless victims of human trafficking, and the front-line workers that face unimaginable darkness to rescue them.

Acknowledgments

I never thought that I would be able to write a book, even less a book about human trafficking. But God has His plans, and so I thank Him first and foremost, for giving me the urge to write this, and for bringing the right people into my life to help me complete it.

This story would never have been written if not for Matthew Friedman, founder and CEO of The Mekong Club. It was his tireless dedication to modern slavery victims that brought this story to the public eye in his seminal book "Where Were You?" That was a book that I could not put down, and contained the seed of the story that you now hold in your hands. Matt encouraged me to elaborate on this story, and provided unceasing support throughout the editing process. He is better than the best mentor I could have imagined or asked for.

There were also a number of friends who were willing to put in time and effort to improve the writing of this amateur writer. My gratitude goes to Geeta Tupps and Alison Stephens, the best English teachers I know, whose educative passion extends beyond the classroom. I am indebted to Quinton Sung, whose writing greatly surpasses my own, yet provided such encouraging and insightful feedback that finally allowed me to consider this book complete. Linda Repetto, Nicholas Wong, Alessandro Riente, Ivan Mak, Shaurye Vardhan, Shelagh Li,

Pearl Yan, John Kim, Shaddy Hanna, Nicole Tanner, and others who may have read this story but forgot to give me feedback; you guys are the best. It's not easy reading 30+ pages of extra-curricular literature (especially when it's a depressing story), but all of you took time for me, and gave such positive and constructive feedback.

I wish I didn't have to write this story, but am eternally grateful for those who have been so supportive throughout the journey.

March 9th, 2010
10:05AM

It started with a phone call—one among the two dozen calls Morris received every day. But to this Burmese humanitarian worker, they meant so much more. Each of them was a woman, a man, a child, who needed desperate help in regaining their freedom.

This phone call was one that changed Morris' life forever.

Ring ring, ring ring, ring ring.

"Hello, this is Morris of the help hotline," he said in Thai. "How can I help you?"

Raspy, shallow breaths. A stifled whimper.

Bad phone connection was common in the middle of bustling Bangkok, so he tried again: "Hello? Hello?"

A female voice, barely a whisper, barely audible, answered in Burmese. "Sir! I have been kidnapped, I need help!" There was an explicit urgency in the tiny voice that Morris had never perceived in any of his previous calls.

His eyebrows furrowed and he switched to Burmese. "Miss, please stay calm, I am here with you. Do you know where you are?"

The voice on the other end—a young girl, it seemed—stuttered through her sobs. "I...I don't know! I can't understand any of the signs...it's all in Thai," she stammered. "I've been in the car for many hours...I don't know where they're taking me! I'm in the toilet, they don't know I have a phone. I need your help..." She broke down, her anguished cries causing Morris' hands to tremble. *Stay calm, stay calm. I must be calm to be able to help her.*

Deep breaths—in and out. That eased the mounting weight in his ribcage, but did nothing for his shaking hands. This was all too sudden, all too new. Like a fresh nightmare. "Try to keep calm, miss," he finally managed to say. "I will help you. What is your name? My name is Morris." He hoped that this semblance of human connection would dilute the unfiltered fear that enclosed their dialogue.

In response, the sobs on the other end abated somewhat. "My name is Mya..." came the reply. It was followed by a sharp intake of breath. "I have to go, they're coming! I'll try to call again—"

"Wait, Mya, let me—" But the line was already dead. "Hello? *Hello?*"

The phone had never felt heavier in his hand as he replaced it on its stand; in fact, his quivering fingers dropped it on the table before he found the cradle. Morris only noticed then that he had been holding his breath, ever muscle in his body rigid with anxiety. *Breathe in, breathe out.* There was a tingling sensation running from his temples all the way down his spine. He shook his head to clear his thoughts, still uncertain what had just happened. He needed help. Turning around in his chair, his mind switched to English. "Jeremy, umm, can you come here a moment? I need your help." His own voice sounded strange to his ears. Speaking several languages in the space of as many minutes was nothing new to him, but this time the language change felt daunting, and it left a bad taste in his mouth.

A stout middle-aged man appeared—Jeremy Moore, their technical advisor. He was a reliable, resourceful man they could always turn to for technical expertise. "I swear, if this is another joke about rebooting your phone, I'm walking outta here." His grin disappeared when he caught Morris' grim expression, his tightly-drawn body.

"Jeremy..." Morris began, coughing to clear the lump in his throat. "I just had a call from a Burmese girl who says she was kidnapped. She's in a car and has no idea where she is, since she can't read the road signs. Before I could get any more information, her phone disconnected." The reality of what he had just experienced hit him then, his words hanging in the air between the two sile⌐ nen. "I...I don't know what to do," he
His listener stood completely still for
aw tight, staring fixedly at Morris.
nost hear the cogs whirring madly
l advisor's brain.

Finally, Morris watched with relief as Jeremy's facial expression transitioned from concern to worry, then resolution. If nothing else, Jeremy could be counted on as a man of planning and action—and this situation definitely called for more than Morris' trademark empathy and listening skills.

Morris ventured a thought, just as much to break the silence as anything else. "Maybe I should just call her back—"

"No!" Jeremy nearly shouted as he grabbed Morris' hand, midway to the phone. "Her captors may find out that she has a cellphone. Who knows what they'd do to her then."

Jeremy took a deep breath, seemingly allowing himself a moment of thought as his eyes settled absentmindedly back on his coworker.

Morris was conscious that his features were not striking, and certainly not those of a stereotypical rescuer: wide face and nose, rounded features, short, jet-black hair, lips always ready to break into a thin—albeit contagious—smile. He knew he was kindhearted—but would that actually help anyone? This phone call, whatever it was, was certainly messing with his own mental clarity.

"We must keep this line of communication open for as long as possible," said Jeremy, breaking Morris' train of thought. The younger man nodded, aware of the enormous mistake he had almost committed.

Another moment of silence passed, both men wrapped in thought, until they decided in unison: "We've got to ask Marg for help."

10:10AM

The office was not large by any measurement, especially considering it belonged to a large international humanitarian organization; funds needed to be kept to a minimum. A small step into the room revealed everything there was to see—three desks, one of them partitioned off to form a makeshift 'room', and cabinets stuffed full of documents, folders and miscellaneous paperwork lining each wall. There were medium-sized windows along one of them, while the other three were blank except for a framed picture of the Thai king and a clock.

At the moment, the scrubby office held its breath, waiting for the response of its ruling authority figure—Margaret Hall, coordinator of the Thailand office. She was in her chair, dressed in her usual loose button-up white shirt, the sleeves rolled up, and dark jeans. Her legs were crossed, fingers forming a triangle in front of her in contemplation. An eyebrow was raised quizzically—not a good sign.

"Let me get this straight. You want to find a kidnapped girl based on this complete *lack* of information?" Morris flinched at the stark honesty in the statement. Like most of Margaret's responses to his suggestions, it contained a staggering amount of rationality, and not a single iota of sympathy. At five foot six, Margaret obviously did not evoke awe and fear from her physique, but what she lacked in build, she more than made up for in attitude and charisma. She was the type of person you would love to work with, but not for. Her two inferiors trembled before her, hoping she would relent.

Gathering his confidence, Jeremy stepped in. "Marg, all we're asking for is some optimism." He cleared his throat, to check if Margaret would allow him to continue. She was silent, so he went on, "From a technical viewpoint, this girl even having a cell phone with her is a miracle, and she might be able to call again. Just give us a chance...we're not asking for much." Not an argument he was probably proud of, Morris thought, not liking their chances.

She mulled over Jeremy's words, jaw clenching and unclenching as if literally chewing the idea. "You guys do remember the last time I risked my job for you, right?" she finally said in an even tone. "The police still aren't talking to me after that botched rescue attempt—it made headlines, remember? They lost face, I lost face, heck, I'm surprised I'm still here!" Jeremy took a half-step back in retreat, clearly remembering all too well the scathing defeat of that event. Morris didn't blame him for the action—he'd already given up even maintaining eye contact with their superior.

Margaret was still for a moment, arms crossed, jaw tight, eyes boring holes in her colleagues' heads. If she only considered their last failed rescue, Morris knew there would be no room for negotiation. But this time, the payoff was surely not so outrageous; it might be a couple hours' worth of effort, a few phone calls, and then *maybe* a police raid or two, Morris quickly calculated. If they failed, no biggie. On the other hand, if they did somehow manage to resolve a cross-border trafficking case...

Margaret sighed, evidently coming to the same conclusion. "I am going to take this risk"—Morris and Jeremy exhaled with relief—"*but* I will only be making tentative calls to prepare relevant contacts for future—*definitive*—updates on her location." That was enough for Morris. More than enough. The victorious duo skittered off to his desk, eager to begin preparations for Mya's next potential call. They were hopeful.

Jeremy, with characteristic vigor, got right down to work. "If she calls again, we'll need to ask simple questions that'll provide us with the necessary information to triangulate her location," he mused, Morris struggling to keep up with all of Jeremy's pointers in writing. "Her answers must be specific; always ask for clarification. Numbers are useless unless we know place names. Landmarks are key. Temples are useless unless they're huge ones, or famous. Stores...hmm...maybe ask her if she recognizes any famous logos? Ugh, no, no, forget that...don't want her to throw Nike, Adidas, or other common advertisements at us. Stick to chain stores, or malls." The list that Jeremy scribbled down was barely legible and growing messier by the second. Morris' was little better.

In frantic moments like this, the American man's quick speech became nearly unintelligible to Morris, who only began to learn English after high school. It was sometimes difficult to keep up with Jeremy, and most of his jokes made no sense to Morris. He enjoyed laughing along anyway. It helped that he had worked as an intern at the office during his university years, which had acclimatized him somewhat to Jeremy and Margaret's American way of communication. Thankfully, this language barrier never got in the way of the two men's friendship; many of their other qualities were too similar for that. Nonetheless, when the situation called for speedy collaboration, Morris was still learning about the nuances of spoken English.

After giving himself time enough to digest Jeremy's barrage of suggestions, Morris made a suggestion of his own. "What if we eavesdropped on her captors through the phone?"

Jeremy's eyes lit up. "That's a brilliant idea! Risky, but brilliant." A final scribble added to the mass of now completely illegible scrawls.

Now all they needed was another call from Mya.

Dec 23, 2009

"You mean girls actually fall for ads like these?"

"Yes, and boys and adults too. Despite rumors of loved ones disappearing, the poor can't afford to miss such opportunities," said Morris. His placid tone belied the gravity of the knowledge that human traffickers often placed ads in local newspapers—inconspicuous ones, promising employment and lucrative pay—to draw people into servitude and exploitation.

Brows creased, Jeremy was clearly unsatisfied with the answer, scratching his head at the newspaper spread out before them. "But these ads are so suspicious, aren't they? I mean, double the average income...no education required...nobody would fall for that, it's too good to be true."

"Jeremy," said Margaret, "what if your family were starving, and you knew you were all going to die soon, and then one day you saw this ad, promising the one solution that could feed everyone?" Jeremy closed his mouth. "Or, to take a less extreme example, what if you could afford an education for your children if only you answered the ad? Without it, your children would grow up in poverty, just as you did. Wouldn't you want the absolute best for them? Besides, these jobs—fishing, waitressing, labor— are perfectly respectable, normal jobs. Would you take the risk, or would you rather spend your entire life regretting not taking it to change your entire future?" Jeremy's stricken expression showed his sudden understanding..

"The issue becomes even more complicated considering the context," added Morris. "Even I have much to learn. Now we must find ways to address it."

For the next two hours, the team racked their brains for plausible solutions. They could either target the traffickers—track them down somehow and arrest them—or else the potential victims...which basically meant the entire population, as Margaret pointed out. Jeremy suggested disseminating educational leaflets to all schools and universities, but the logistics would be difficult to manage, not to mention requiring considerable cooperation from institutions and government bodies. Quite the nightmare, Margaret assured them. They then toyed with the idea of calling the numbers on the ads to reach the traffickers, and then...well, what could they do? There was no phone tracking, no GPS, no way to use the numbers to their advantage. What good would verbal warnings or threats do?

"What if we do what the traffickers do?" suggested Morris, rousing Jeremy from his hair ruffling and Margaret from seething frustration.

"What do you mean?"

"Well, they're posting ads. We could do the same." Struck by the simplicity of the idea, Margaret sat down and crumpled up the note-filled paper she had been scribbling on, starting on a fresh sheet. Jeremy sat and squinted at

Morris.

"Go on," she said.

Morris thought for a moment. "They post ads about jobs, since of course everyone wants them. Maybe they know the risks, maybe they don't. We can post ads in the same newspapers..."

"...telling people to call *us* instead," Margaret scribbled furiously, relishing the plan.

"Our ad can say something like, 'If you're thinking about responding to that lucrative job ad, please call us first'. And we can include our own hotline in the ad. That way, we get to know who the people are and maybe even help them in our own way."

Jeremy cleared his throat, frowning. "I hate to rain on the parade, but can we backtrack just a tiny bit here? First, we don't have a hotline. Second, we don't have enough funds for an ad campaign of that breadth. Third, and most important, doesn't the whole plan sound sort of...simple and naïve? No offense," he said, glancing at Morris. They lapsed back into silence, chewing on Jeremy's perfectly valid questions.

"Okay," said Margaret, "I'm not making any spur-of-the-moment promises here, but about the funding and the hotline—let me worry about that, it's not a concern. What Jeremy mentioned about the simplicity of the idea though..." She looked at Morris.

"I know how this may sound to you," began Morris, "but the locals aren't dumb. Just desperate to survive, and we'd risk everything to provide for our family, our parents, children, even our village. This plan may be simple, but it's not naïve. I believe success does not depend on a complex plan; it calls for seeing the problem and addressing it. Let's try with this, and then see how it goes."

The expression on Jeremy's face had softened, the faintest glimmer of hope in his expression. "Well, you're the local," he said. "If we can't trust you, who can we trust?" Margaret nodded, sealing the deal and ending the meeting. Everyone gathered their notes up and pulled out their laptops. There was work to be done and obstacles to demolish, and Margaret was obviously itching to get started.

"Really think this'll work?" Jeremy asked Morris, back at their desks. This time, the question spoke of a need for reassurance rather than doubt.

Morris leaned back, hands clasped behind his head, gazing into the distance. "To be honest, I don't know, but that's not my concern. Knowing doesn't matter; doing does."

Jeremy chuckled. "And here I was thinking I was the man of action around here. I have much to learn from you, Morris."

It took two months for Margaret to secure the necessary funding and call in technicians to set up the dedicated hotline. By tacit agreement, they ordained Morris the hotline operator, if only because there were no other candidates. To their surprise—even Morris'—calls started to come in. At first there were only one or two a week, usually teenagers tempted to make a quick buck in the cities. However, even victims of the trafficking ads themselves soon reached out, sharing their stories, asking for help. Within a few months, the number of calls exponentially increased by word of mouth among victims and would-be victims of trafficking. With some amazement, Jeremy calculated that they received more than a hundred calls in the first six months of operation.

Of course, along with the victims, traffickers also noticed their ad, and they were understandably upset. Threats started to come in, these promising violence, torture and death. Morris was upset at first, Jeremy scared out of his wits, but Margaret pointed out a fact that allayed their fears somewhat: they now had the traffickers' phone numbers. Needless to say, the police were surprised at the list of numbers Margaret handed them; one that constantly grew in length and diversity, suggesting large cross-border criminal activity.

The hotline turned out to be most valuable operation the team had ever conceived, causing Margaret and Jeremy to nickname Morris 'the Samaritan'. After explaining the story to him, he fell in love with it.

March 9th, 2010
12:45PM

The wait was excruciating.

Every second felt like an hour, the tense anticipation weighing heavily on the three staff members in the office. Morris sat with his head in his hands, staring unblinkingly at the phone, willing it to ring. Jeremy put up more of a semblance of work, though it was obvious from his idiosyncratic typing that he wasn't getting any work done. Margaret seemed to be her usual productive self, but her heart was clearly with Morris, praying for the second call. The air itself hummed with tension, as if infused with gaseous caffeine.

Ring ring, ring ring.

Even though he had been waiting for the sound for over two hours, Morris jumped when the phone finally rang. Jeremy made a mad dash to join him.

"Hello! This is Morris!" he cried out in Burmese, abandoning the protocol to speak Thai.

"Mr. Morris..." the familiar timid voice said, before breaking down into piteous sobs, "I don't know if I can call you again. When will you come rescue me?" The sobs became uncontrolled crying, sending sympathetic shivers down Morris' spine. It didn't take an acute understanding of the language for his colleagues to recognize the fear in her words. Morris fought to contain his emotions—there was work to be done.

"Mya, I promise I will do all I can to rescue you. Don't give up, okay?" He waited for a murmured "Yes" from her before proceeding. "Now I have to ask you some questions to see where you are. Did you see any large landmarks since your last stop?" The crying stopped, followed by a slight pause.

"I...I think I saw some mountains..." she stuttered.

"Good job, Mya! How many mountains were there?" Morris could hardly contain the excitement in his voice. As he wrote 'MOUNTAINS' on his notebook, Jeremy and Margaret leaned in, their faces etched in concentration.

"Many mountains, all in a line." Morris scribbled down the details madly in English for his peers, 'LINE OF MOUNTS'.

"How many, Mya? Can you guess how many there were?"

"Six...no, seven...no...I don't remember!" A cry broke out, which brought Morris back to his empathic senses. *Slow down! She's just as lost as you are...guide her slowly, slowly.* Jeremy had picked up on the words for "six" and "seven", and began to search online for mountain ranges.

"It's okay, Mya! You're doing great!" he reassured her. "We're much closer to finding you now. Did the line of mountains face you or point away from you?"

"They faced me...in a line." More writing, 'FACED HER IN LINE'.

He suddenly remembered a crucial question. "Mya! Were you looking out from the left or the right side of the car?"

"I..I...don't know..." she said, hesitating, then drew in a sharp breath, "It was the left! I saw the mountains from the left." Morris almost slammed the desk in elation. This was good, this was *so* good, but they still needed many more details. He almost forgot to write down 'LEFT OF CAR'.

"And were they close or far away?" he continued.

"They were close." Yes, yes, this was progress! *Close.* They had probably been a range of sandstone hills, one among the many dotted throughout northern Thailand. Jeremy already had Google Maps opened on his laptop, searching for highways or roads that ran close to mountain ranges. Morris, desperate to continue this flow of clues, prodded: "Mya, you are doing so well. Did you see anything special along the way? Something that stood out?" A moment's pause, which felt like an eternity.

Finally, hesitantly, Mya replied: "We passed by many sunflowers. They were beautiful..." Sunflowers? They couldn't have asked for a more unique landmark. Jeremy suddenly punched the air in triumph as he shoved his laptop at Morris. The highway running through the Sabari province—about an hour and thirty minutes' drive from Bangkok—was famous for its sunflower fields.

"Sir, where are they taking me—" sudden silence, interrupted by a man's voice shouting for

Mya to hurry up. "Find me, please, or they will hurt me again! Rescue me, please!"

"Wait, waitwaitwaitwait! Mya, leave your cellphone on in your pocket!"

Silence. They didn't know if their message had been heard. They could only hope it was.

Morris gritted his teeth with frustration; they *needed* to get more information from her kidnappers! They now knew which highway the kidnappers took to enter Bangkok, but not a clue as to their present location. Without knowing when —or if—Mya could make the next call, they needed solid leads, and fast. From the corner of his eye he could see Jeremy lean back in his chair, frustration clear on his features.

Just as he was about to hang up, he heard a muffled voice speaking in Thai. "...Next time you take so long, we'll make you pee in a bag! Get in the van!" Either the speaker did not know Mya spoke Burmese, or he did not care. Morris immediately gestured for Jeremy to keep quiet as he pressed the speaker button on the phone. From her desk, Margaret watched intently, fingers poised over her own phone, ready to call her contacts in the Royal Thai Police, the Ministry of Justice...anybody and everybody on her list.

The muffled voices now broadcasting in their office were gruff and...young? Morris could not stomach the idea of young men kidnapping their peers for profit. He wished his Thai was better; the men spoke quickly and used a lot of slang. It was tough trying to translate what they said in real time, and Jeremy and Margaret soon gave up with their limited Thai, fixing their attention instead on Morris' facial expressions and occasional translation notes. The overheard conversation flitted from one mundane topic to the next for ten painful minutes. With each passing remark, there seemed less hope that they would ever mention any bit of useful information.

"...Seriously? Another Central Plaza? They're popping up everywhere." Morris wrote CENTRAL PLAZA on his notebook, causing Jeremy to sit hurriedly upright in his chair, fingers flying across his laptop, searching for locations of the well-known shopping mall chain. It was just one of the thousands in Thailand, but progress was progress.

"All this driving's making me famished. Where are we eating?"

"You're always hungry!" the other voice laughed. "Turn left on Yaowarat road, I'm craving some KFC." The listeners had concluded that this voice belonged to the non-driving captor; his voice was slightly younger, higher in pitch and with more of a colloquial slur in his words. Morris added to his list, 'YAOWARAT ROAD, KFC.'

"What's with you and Western food? You never want to eat Thai food. Hey...are you sure this is the right—" Suddenly, the line went silent. Morris and Jeremy looked at each other, eyes wide with surprise.

What had happened to the phone...and what had happened to Mya?

12:50PM

Margaret walked over to see if she could offer any help, but was reduced to silence when she found her coworkers mute and motionless.

Jeremy cleared his throat and broke the silence. "Let's not worry too much. Let's not assume the worst. Maybe the battery died, or she accidentally hung up..." He trailed off. The possibilities were endless, but none afforded them any hope. He turned to Morris, "What were they saying before the line died?" But Morris just continued to stare.

Margaret pursed her lips. Tough love was her specialty. "Morris, Jeremy." They turned their heads, ever so slightly, toward her. "You know I took a risk by allowing you to focus on finding this girl. I took a risk based on nothing but your optimism. Nothing. But now that you have something to work with, you give up?" She shook her head emphatically. "I'm not going to let you off that easily. Go wash your face, do jumping jacks, whatever. But I want 110% from you in five minutes. I didn't hire you to sulk." And with that, she stalked off.

Morris' eyes began to focus again as Margaret's pep talk sank in. Jeremy, who wore a look of apprehension throughout her talk, also began to nod his head in agreement, repeating to himself the technical crux of her message that spoke to him. "110%, 110%, 110%." With a deep breath, both men came to the same conclusion—this was no time to let fear get the better of them.

"So," began Jeremy, gathering his thoughts as his voice regained its vigor, "range of limestone hills, KFC, Yaowarat road, Central Plaza. You look online for KFC branch locations and Central Plaza locations. Mark down the ones that are close together. I'll mark down the limestone hills and find Yaowarat road, figure out which side of the mountains they're on...no!" Morris jumped at his sudden outburst. "Can't believe we forgot to ask her that!" He angrily opened Google Maps on his laptop and began his self-assigned tasks, venting his annoyance through action. Morris could not have asked for a better companion, whose presence and pragmatism anchored their morale.

He couldn't help but express his gratitude: "Hey, Jeremy...thank you."

Jeremy could only give a rueful smile in return.

1:13PM

Four.

There were four areas that contained a KFC, a Central Plaza and a Yaowarat street. Statistically improbable, but apparently luck was not on their side. They stared at the online map with four large red circles, each containing all of the landmarks. The circles were nowhere near each other. Four never sounded like a larger number. They needed help—someone who knew the lay of the land and was fluent in the language. It was taking far too long for the three of them alone to search everything online and interpret the kidnappers' Thai. Morris and Margaret called their local contacts; most were at work, but two agreed to come in after realizing the urgency of the situation.

To make a difficult situation all but impossible, Jeremy exploded with a staggering realization: *"We forgot to ask her what type of car she was in."* He then calmly took a red marker, pulled up his shirt sleeve and wrote a single word across his entire arm—'CAR'. Then he wrote it again. And again. And again. Then he threw the marker across the room. Morris and Margaret exchanged glances—they had never seen the amiable Jeremy so angry before. With his face buried deep in his hands, Jeremy could be heard mumbling, "Technical advisor...technical advisor? What are you?" Two minutes passed, then five, then ten. The self-abasement continued.

Eventually, Margaret could stand no more. She put a hand on the sullen man's shoulder, "Jeremy, it's time to move on. It's time to do your job." Perhaps it was her choice of words, or perhaps her timing—whatever it was, it brought Jeremy to his feet, where he uttered a single sentence before walking out of the office: "Maybe I'm not fit to do my job anymore." Their gazes followed him out. They knew better than to try and make him stay. God knew how close they all were to their limit for frustration.

Jeremy eventually returned, as wordless as he had left, much to the relief of his peers. It didn't matter where he went, or that he looked just as sullen as before. All that mattered was that he had chosen to return. Back at his seat, with one sleeve still rolled up past his elbow, he watched over the phone with a look of grim determination.

Without sufficient information to mobilize the police, they resorted back to the suspenseful wait around Morris' desk. Waiting for the Thai locals to arrive. Waiting for Mya to call. Waiting for anything.

Dec 24, 2008

His name was Kasem. As his name suggested, his parents had wanted nothing but pure happiness for him.

Nobody called him by that name now. He was known by the network as Romeo for his good looks, his charisma, his charm and his way with girls. Almost every glimpse proved to be love at first sight.

Everybody loved Kasem—the brothels, the pimps, the mamasans. Everybody but the girls, of course, once they found out who and what he truly was. Putting his charm to use, Kasem's job for the past two years had been to travel around different rural villages and seduce young girls, selling them to brothels in wealthy cities like Bangkok. There was no end to the demand, and fortunately for him, none to the supply either. The job gave him a sense of power, of independence, allowing him to support his family back home and himself. It was more than most village boys could ever dream of.

Wherever he went, a sea of nameless faces surrounded him, tear-streaked, smeared with makeup. Kasem had long lost track of how many girls he had sold, how many hearts he had broken. What did it matter? To destroy the second life was the same as the first, and every one after that just made his heart number, his conscience quieter. Insomnia was a side effect he had learned to live with.

There was always only ever one dream, one nightmare, which stayed with him throughout the years. In it, he revisited the first girl he ever seduced. He would never forget her name— Lawan, beautiful—or her face, a perfect half-moon. Kasem had marveled at how easily she fell for him, how readily her family let him take her away—begged him, even, to bring her to the city, to give her the life they could not. There had never been a photo taken with more smiling faces than their wedding picture, with her twenty relatives crowding around him: grateful, relieved, happy. Blessed.

On the drive to the city, Lawan, now officially Kasem's wife, placed a simple red string bracelet into his hand, closing his fingers around it. "Wear it," she had told him. "It will give you luck. My parents got it for me from the temple, and now I have found you, so I do not need any more luck." Then she had fallen asleep on his shoulder, completely trusting. How pure she had been. Kasem had needed to clench his fist to quell the tremors then. That was where the dream-memory became nightmare.

Kasem would look down to see that, instead of the bracelet, he held a blood vessel connected to Lawan's wrist, pulsing and glistening and alive. Lawan would pull on it, beginning to cry and scream, until it ripped open along the length of her arm and into her chest. Blood and tears would take over his vision as his wife ripped out her own beating heart, offering it to him with both hands. That was when he always woke up, shouting or crying, his body racked with uncontrollable trembling.

The worst part of it was that Kasem could not quite bring himself to remove the bracelet. He would stroke his wrist to find it there, had worn it every day since, long after he locked the brothel door on his first wife's questioning eyes. He never asked himself why he kept it, the string now frayed and the color dulled.

Kasem swore under his breath. There was always something about the open road between rural and urban areas he hated. Too much time to think. It was a long trip across the border from Yangon to Bangkok. Of all his hunting grounds, Yangon district was a favorite, developed with decent infrastructure and other comforts, the smooth roads ripe with guileless girls. Beautiful, too; a fact that had made things harder in the beginning, but was more pleasant now.

"What you thinking about, man? Stop falling asleep and keep me company." Sakda's gruff voice brought Kasem out of his reverie, back into the rattling van his friend was driving through the fading light.

"You don't need my company," Kasem replied, "you can talk to yourself good enough, I've seen you do it."

Sakda scowled at him, "Don't be like that. Talk with me. Don't want me driving into a ditch, yeah?"

Every time depression overtook him, Kasem was thankful for his best friend and driver, Sakda, who preferred to call himself Kasem's partner in crime. Their banter was a welcome distraction.

"Long way to drive this time," Kasem agreed, rubbing his eyes. "I sure miss Bangkok though."

"You mean you miss the girls there."

"You're one to talk. I bet you have every disease there is." Kasem slapped his face to wake himself up a little, then rolled down the window, taking a few deep breaths. "Let's just get this over with," he said, irritation now brewing. They should never had gone for drinks at that new bar. Then Sakda wouldn't have gotten drunk; then the pretty little girl wandering the street wouldn't have caught his eye; then they wouldn't have had to kidnap her. Kasem hated using force. Besides, kidnappings were nothing but trouble, drawing unnecessary attention and risk.

Most of all, newlywed wives didn't cry in the car, unlike kidnapped girls.

"I have a bad feeling about this girl...what's her name again?"

Sakda scoffed, "You know I don't do names, man. Bad for business. You shouldn't either, if you want to work as long as I have."

Kasem grimaced and muttered to himself, "Ma...mon...Mya?" A fist landed on his arm.

"Whatever it is, I don't want to know," said Sakda. Kasem looked out the window, the sunflower fields on either side dancing with the wind and golden sunlight, breathtaking in their beauty. Even so, he found himself unable to smile.

His name was Kasem, but he no longer felt happiness. They called him Romeo.

March 9th, 2010
1:42PM

Morris' desk had always been the tidiest among his colleagues, reflecting his uncomplicated personality—a characteristic that endeared him to everyone he worked with. But with the urgency and sheer pressure of the day's events, he had completely cleared off the desk in the most uncharacteristic manner, wildly stuffing everything into any available cabinet and drawer. Now all that remained was his phone. It had become the unforeseen anchor to his soul, the only thread connecting him to this unknown young girl. Mya's life and death were contained within this mundane device, and so Morris both hated and clung to it.

Almost an hour had passed since the last call, so the silent trio were startled from their daze by footsteps in the hallway outside. The two Thai helpers had arrived.

The newcomers introduced themselves as Aat and Chariya. Aat was a gentle, soft-spoken young man in his mid-twenties, friendly yet reserved. Since he worked as a driver, he knew the area well. Chariya was in her early thirties, tall and slim. She shared Aat's subdued demeanor, yet her cheerfulness shone through her ready smiles. What pleased Morris the most was that she was fluent in both Thai and Burmese, allowing her assistance in talking with

Mya and eavesdropping on the kidnappers. All in all, the two newcomers brought with them a sense of serenity and normalcy, rejuvenating the forlorn office atmosphere.

They were filled in on Mya's situation and what their respective roles would be. Aat was obviously a people-person, assuring the team that his contact network covered most major retailers and malls. Thanks to him, they would be able to have eyes on the ground at Mya's possible locations—a huge advantage that brought momentary tears of joy to Jeremy's eyes. He and Aat instantly became the perfect division. Chariya, on the other hand, excelled at translation and communication with youth, naturally developed through her work as a youth counsellor at a local NGO. Morris was relieved to know that he would not have to struggle to understand the kidnappers' Thai anymore. Chariya would also be able to better teach him how to comfort Mya in her distress.

As the new teams settled into their roles, planning for the next call, Margaret sat back for the first time in three hours, obviously relishing the camaraderie that was blossoming in the soil of despair.

For the first time, they felt *hopeful*.

2:31PM

Ring ring, ring ring.

The team, who had grown numb and wilted with waiting, were shocked wide awake. Morris scrambled for the phone.

"Hello!" What he really wanted to do was shout into the receiver, telling Mya that it was okay, that they were trying everything they could to save her, that he would never give up. But it might have been someone else in need of help, so he had to revert to protocol, speaking in Thai. When he heard the familiar shallow breathing on the other end, he almost choked on his excitement, throwing a smile at his expectant team. Jeremy shot his arm into the air, fervently displaying the word 'CAR' still written on it.

"Mr. Morris...I don't know if I can call again, why are you taking so long, why...?" Her voice choked up. Try as he did, Morris' voice fared no better.

"Mya...I...we're doing everything we can. We—" Here he had to hold back a sob of his own, pushing down his emotions, "We're making progress! We need to know what kind of vehicle you're in. Is it a car or a van? What color is it? Do you know the license plate number?" Chariya gestured for him to slow down; they had to give Mya time to collect her emotions and memories. He gave her a nod and took a deep breath, attempting to calm himself.

To his relief, the cries subsided. "It's a white van...they keep me locked in the back," she said.

"I'm sorry, I can't remember the license plate number..." She broke off into repeated murmurs of "I'm sorry, I'm sorry." Chariya shook her head and sniffed. This was likely beyond anything she had anticipated when Margaret brought her in.

"It's okay, Mya, it's okay!" Morris reassured her in the most heartening tone he could muster as he wrote 'WHITE VAN' in his notebook. "That's all the information we need for now. We'll search out some possible locations. Mya...Mya...?" But her murmuring had given way to uncontrollable crying and stammered apologies, heavy with remorse at a situation that was not her fault. Morris knew that she needed some light, something to hold on to. He had an idea.

"Mya, can you tell me where you're from? I'm from Bago, in Myanmar."

"...Yangon is my home," Mya eventually managed to reply through her sobs.

That made sense. Despite being the most developed region of the country, the location of the Yangon division made it a hotspot for cross-border human traffickers.

"And your family?" Morris continued. "Tell me about them, Mya." He had to tread carefully here. The line between loss and hope was thin, and he had to keep her thoughts positive. Beside him, Chariya nodded.

"My family is small...there is my pa, my ma, my older brother..." she replied, still sniffing. "They all love me so much. We are poor, but they give me everything. They wanted me to have a better life outside the village..." As the tears returned in full force, Morris could hear her self-reproach. In her mind, she had let her family down, bringing dishonor to them in return for their love and care. It pained Morris to hear a victim blaming herself—a heartbreaking phenomenon he had witnessed among many other victims. He had to lead her to greener pastures.

"Mya, remember those mountains that you saw earlier? They remind you of your village, don't they?" A wild guess, for sure, but he was grasping at anything that could buoy her spirit.

"Yes," whispered Mya. "We had beautiful mountains around our village. In the spring there were so many colorful flowers everywhere." Her voice took on a faraway tone, as if she was looking at the rural scenery in her mind's eye. "My brother would take me to the loveliest spots in the forest. Sometimes I made flower necklaces for him, but he doesn't like to wear them." Her laugh was small and shaky, but it sent a wave of warmth through him. "He thinks wearing flowers is for girls!" Mya continued. Morris couldn't help but laugh along with her. Beside him, Chariya was all smiles as well.

Knowing there might not be a better chance, he ventured: "Mya, your family still loves you so much." He paused and willed his voice to be more persuasive. "They understand that this was not your fault. You haven't let them down, Mya. Trust me on that, okay?"

There was a brief pause as he heard her wipe her tears—then her still, small voice again: "I trust you." That simple expression of faith hit home. If there had been any shred of doubt in this operation so far, it had disintegrated at the sound of those three simple words.

"Never forget that they love you!" He emphasized, wiping the sudden tears from his eyes. "Mya, I promise you that I'll never give up on you," he asserted. "You must promise me not to give up either. Now, you must keep the phone on so that we can hear what the bad people say, okay?"

"Okay...I have to go now, please hurry!" The rustling of the cell phone being snuck away. The muffled sounds of a door opening, then men's voices, a car door opening and closing.

Once again, Morris put the phone on speaker mode, Margaret, Jeremy, Aat and Chariya huddling around it with notebooks and laptops in their hands, hungry for any new information. In response to Chariya's written translations, there was not a single dry eye in the room from the emotional phone call, but they were all business now.

The road trip conversation resumed, and before long took a favorable turn. "...So many temples in this area. Did you know? My parents actually wanted me to be a monk." This confession from one of the captors was met with raucous laughter from the other.

"You? A monk?" the other laughed. "If only your parents could see what you do for a living now!" Morris, Chariya and Aat winced at the irony, and the apparent nonchalance in the speaker's response. Morris did not forget to scribble down, 'HIGH DENSITY OF TEMPLES';

Aat jotted down a few locations as well. "Check out that huge temple! Maybe you can work there, haha!" Another note, 'LARGE TEMPLE'. Jeremy and Margaret set to work on their laptops. After a few more back-and-forths, they lapsed into silence. The office quintet was silent as well, barely daring to breath.

"Turn left at the next street." Five pairs of ears perked up at the foreshadowing of a critical clue, even the two Americans understanding the basic Thai, everyone's pens poised. Margaret's hand gripped her cellphone tighter.

"No, no, I'm sure it's the one after that...Sathon road, not Khaosan road." Mad scribbling ensued—this information had considerably narrowed their search area. Beads of perspiration lined Jeremy's forehead. Aat peered at his notes like a bloodhound straining to begin the hunt.

"You're right for once," the driver's voice grunted. A few minutes of silence elapsed. "How much do you think they'll pay for this one?"

"She looks like at least 20,000 baht to me...maybe even 30,000 if they're in a good mood." The young men chuckled, as though they were merely anticipating a good meal or a new phone. Those who understood the dialogue grimaced in disgust.

Then came another major clue as one of the captors excitedly hollered, "Let's have a celebration at the Spicy Nightclub!" Aat perked up at the mention of this location, scribbling down a name and phone number in his notebook. The others looked at him with curiosity, but were afraid to speak with the phone on speaker mode.

Without warning—yet with frustrating familiarity—the line went dead.

2:50PM

This time, the office quintet allowed themselves only a moment of still surprise, after which they immediately burst into action, each to their own task. The atmosphere was electric.

Aat revealed that one of his friends worked at Spicy Nightclub, and dashed out of the office to call him. Jeremy lunged for his laptop, marking down areas with a high density of temples, looking out for especially large temples. Meanwhile, Chariya and Margaret searched for the two streets mentioned by the kidnappers. They also referred to the previous areas that were marked down, checking to see which ones were within driving distance of the newest street names. Morris ran outside to find Aat to ask him for the location of the nightclub. Miraculously, they had narrowed down two tentative locations within ten minutes. This was the breakthrough they had needed to mobilize the police, and Margaret wasted no time in making a call to the nearest station.

She provided a brief summary of Mya's plight, then a description of the van, the nightclub and the street names; indolently, the police agreed to send out patrol cars. Margaret let out a shout of exultation and pumped her fists in the air, bringing a smile to everyone's lips. After further calls from the team, a number of NGOs joined their effort with their own cars. Jeremy and Morris couldn't help but grin at

Margaret's rapid speech on every phone call, surprised that anyone could make out what she was saying (or as Jeremy called it, rapping). His working theory was that nobody ever understood 100% of what Margaret said, but nobody dared ask for clarification.

Gone was the air of helplessness, the stench of hopelessness; the office pulsated with fresh energy. They had information, they had search teams, they had *hope*. True, the odds were not in their favor. But the fact that there was a *chance*—even if only a slight one—changed everything. For the first time in the past six hours, Morris, Jeremy and Margaret could breathe again. The newcomers, who had only seen the forlorn trio under stress up until then, marveled at the change.

After all was said and done, they settled down to wait, hoping that the police would be able to find the van, and Mya still inside it.

3:06PM

Mya called again, catching everyone off guard. She had never made a call in such quick succession. Drinks were spilled, people quickly summoned from their bathroom breaks. Within fifteen seconds, the office went from complete standstill to battlefield command tent. Morris could see Chariya being careful to observe each team member, probably making sure they weren't about to burn out from the rollercoaster events of the past few hours.

He picked up the phone gingerly, not sure what to expect from such an unexpected call. "Hello?" There was no response but ambient car sounds—the occasional bump in the road, the creaking of the chassis, faint radio music. The office team immediately held their breath, realizing that Mya had called them not to talk, but to try and provide them with more information from her captors. Morris clapped his hand over his mouth and put the phone on speaker, then took a few deep breaths. Chariya put a comforting hand on his shoulder. In such a situation, every action, every word, meant everything. Jeremy reached out to press the mute button on the phone, but the indicator light did nothing—they would have to be absolutely silent from now on, not knowing whether Mya had muted the phone on her end.

Knowing that the police search was underway, the team leaned in, anticipating the rapturous sound of sirens. Morris was dying to explain their breakthrough to Mya, to include her in their pent-up expectation, but the cost of the captors discovering her cellphone was far too high.

Sudden footsteps could be heard, and in rushed Aat, excitement plastered on his fact. "Guys, guys, my friend at the night—" Before he could finish his sentence, Jeremy had cleared the distance between his desk and the door and charged headlong into the young man, bowling him over like a fleshy cannonball. The others had not even had time to register their surprise. A stupefied Aat groaned in pain on the floor as Jeremy clamped his hand over the other's mouth. Everyone could only stare in complete shock; first at Aat's untimely appearance, then at Jeremy's reaction. A split second later, their attention was back on the phone. Had the captors heard him? Had they blown the call?

All they could hear now was silence. Deafening silence. No car sounds, no radio, no creaking, no talking. No Mya.

The line was dead.

3:08PM

Aat remained on the floor while Chariya tended to his bruised head. On the other side of the office, Margaret gave Jeremy hell for his reckless action.

"What the *hell* were you thinking, Jeremy?"

Jeremy sheepishly replied, "I...I...we couldn't have them—"

But Margaret lifted a hand. "Yes, of course I knew *that*. But why the—"

"I couldn't have just sat there!" he protested.

Margaret was gaining steam, voice rising. "But that doesn't justify your *violence*, Jeremy! How could you think that—" Jeremy, however, was also gaining momentum of his own, rising from his chair.

"*I had to do something!*" Jeremy burst out. "We all know I was the only one who did something about it!" His voice took on an accusatory tone. "What? Would you have preferred it if Mya's phone was discovered? Is that what you want?"

By now, all eyes were on him. Margaret's typically unfaltering gaze shifted to the side. They all understood his anger—in a way, he was the manifestation of their collective outrage, giving voice to their unspeakable emotions.

"What was I to do? Come on, tell me!" Jeremy continued, his voice gaining pitch and volume. "We've been seeing this happen over and over again. Don't act like this is new to you.

So, what have you been doing about it? Tell me! It's because of people like *you* that girls like Mya get taken and eaten alive!" He pointed a shaking finger at a stunned Margaret, "It's because of *people...like...you!*" Margaret averted her gaze, as did the others.

Morris made his way to the trembling and red-faced Jeremy, who seemed to have drained his emotional cask to its dregs and was now muttering to himself. "It's because you don't do *anything...*" He collapsed back into his chair, uttering one last murmured accusation, barely a whisper: "It's because of people like me...people like me..." Morris put a hand on his friend's shoulder, his tears mirroring Jeremy's. The silence following his outburst accentuated his words. Margaret excused herself to no one in particular and strode to the washroom as Chariya continued to tend to Aat, sniffing quietly.

Laying exactly where Jeremy had left him, Aat remained motionless, staring at the ceiling. Morris noticed the tears welling in his eyes. Under the still facade, Morris knew guilt would be writhing and seething like a flaming snake, tearing at his insides. He knew it because Morris had felt it before too, at his failure to help those most in need. He didn't need to know Aat well to see that he was questioning himself about what he had done, how he could have been so careless—perhaps even wishing that Jeremy had pummeled him, beating some sense into his head. He remained there on the floor, seemingly unwilling to get up and face the consequences of his mistake.

The office once again plunged into despondency as the oppressive silence rushed in to fill the void. Each grieving individual was a separate room with locked doors, to which nobody had the keys.

3:15PM

Margaret managed to run to the bathroom, blindly barge into a stall, lock it, and crouch down to the floor before breaking down. The tears flowed freely for the first time in many years as violent sobs racked her body. The greater the emotional suppression, the greater the breakdown—and Margaret's inhibition had been protracted indeed. The strain of the past six hours had ground her stamina to dust, dealing blow after relentless blow to her morale. They had warned her about the pitfalls of humanitarian work and the signs of burnout, but never did she imagine that it would happen to her in a cramped bathroom stall in Thailand.

After fifteen minutes of unabated tears, her anguish morphed into self-reproach—something she had perfected throughout her life. This entire situation was her fault, a consequence of her delayed action, her incompetence, her inability to coordinate an effective search and rescue mission, her ineptitude in overseeing her own staff—

Her thoughts were interrupted by a tentative knock on the door, followed by Chariya's voice. "Margaret, are you there?"

She made no reply, but hastily wiped her face as clean as possible.

Chariya was clearly not one to give up, "Margaret, can I come in?" Margaret wondered at the Thai woman's ability to sound gentle and firm at the same time, making her statement both a request and an assertion. Her footsteps stopped in front of Margaret's stall.

"Margaret, I know how you feel," she began in a compassionate tone. "We all..." She sighed deeply, "I think we all feel the same way." Margaret bit her lips as she noticed the tremor in Chariya's voice. *Don't make me start crying again. Don't you dare.*

Chariya continued. "You're putting so much responsibility on your shoulders. But it's time to stop blaming yourself." Margaret shook her head vehemently, knowing that it was not so. Mercy was reserved for those who deserved it, forgiveness for those who earned it. That was just how life worked.

"There's no need to make it about you. It's about Mya. Let's share that responsibility..." Suddenly Chariya started sobbing herself, struggling to speak through her tears. "Blame the kidnappers...blame our culture...blame our corruption...*just not yourself!*" With that final plea, she sank to the floor, the weight of her own sense of guilt obvious, belying her words. On opposite sides of the stall door, both curled up on the ground, they shared their mutual grief that had finally taken too much mental toll.

Five quiet minutes later, Margaret opened the stall door, little trace of her tears left and her expression set with a look of grim resolve. She wrapped her arms around Chariya in a quick embrace, muttered a "thank you" and proceeded to wash her face. A slightly confused Chariya followed suit, clearly unsure whether this signified restoration or aggravation. Margaret was not sure she knew herself—but that did not matter, not now. As with everything else they had to deal with this day, only time would tell.

4:00PM

The police gave up after an hour.

They managed to find a van that matched the description parked at the Spicy Nightclub, but it was not involved in any illegal activity. Since the nightclub was closed, the kidnappers had probably stopped at another unknown location. The NGO search teams had scouted nearby bars and nightclubs recommended by Aat, but also came up empty. Nobody ventured to ask Margaret and Chariya about their puffy red eyes when they returned from the washroom—everyone understood. With the fresh disappointment, the team was dejected beyond words, slumped in a loose circle around Morris' desk; even Aat had finally roused himself enough to join the group. Margaret, however, fumed silently.

Within ten minutes of receiving the news from the police, without a word to anyone, she stormed out of the office. Chariya had wanted to follow, but Morris reassured her that Margaret was the type of person who simply had to do what she had to do. Whatever it was, she would be better off doing *something* other than sit around.

Once again, they were back to waiting—for Margaret to return, for Mya to call, for a miracle to occur. A miracle that felt like it had fizzled into complete impossibility long, long ago.

4:15PM

Margaret had never felt this useless in her twenty years of experience as a humanitarian worker. Known in her field for her resourcefulness and influence, she rarely encountered any obstacle that could not be overcome by a few phone calls or a dinner party. Politics and bureaucratic etiquette were her forte. After all these years, she had finally met her match.

Ironically, it was a case that would not make headlines nor win her any accolades. Even so, it had struck a chord in her heart. Mya's kidnapping was a monster that tore out Margaret's pride, her beating heart, and was devouring it in front of her, goading her, mocking her. She was helpless to lift even a finger to vindicate herself. Experience meant *nothing*, networks meant *nothing*, influence meant *nothing*. She meant nothing.

Like all the major childhood memories she harbored, this self-deprecation fueled her drive like gasoline on fire; in this way, every weakness became a strength. This time it was something more, something beyond her personal sense of powerlessness. As Chariya had said, this time it wasn't about *her*. Not anymore.

She had stormed out of the office and headed straight for the nearest police station, sorrow-fueled resolution driving her tired body. She barely noticed the fifteen-minute walk in drizzly weather. The perplexed policeman had hesitantly brought her to their chief, who had then listened to her summarized account with mild interest. She ended with the demand that they station police at the popular nightclubs and bars in the area. In their culturally polite way, he had said no. She had tried a softer approach, but it met with the same response. A veiled threat did no better—in fact, it got her kicked out of the police station. *Great, now I've even managed to antagonize this entire division.* Experience had taught her that anger and impatience got one nowhere, but she had not been this frustrated in many years, and at the moment, her seething anger was cathartic.

For the first few blocks on the way back to the office, her mind was consumed with resentment. The antipathy, the ignorance, the inhumanity of it all drove her insane. Contrary to her training, she began to see this place, this people, as full of darkness. The heartless kidnappers were supported by corrupt police, and the ignorant public refused to acknowledge the atrocities happening right beneath their noses. She shook her head at the swelling indignation within, jaw tight, fists clenched. But a fire can only burn so long without sustenance. Within another block, the strong, confident Margaret, who always had a spring in her step and a fire in her eyes, was reduced to a shadow, the fire faded to smoldering disappointment.

"Miss, miss!" An unfamiliar voice called out in English from behind, startling Margaret from her reverie. She stared warily as a young Thai man ran up to her, slightly out of breath. "My name is Decha," he explained. "I'm a police officer at the station you were just in. I would really like to help you to find that young girl."

There was a sincerity in his eyes that brought Margaret back from her inner hell. The frown faded from her face, bringing a look of relief from Decha. "Please, let me help," he added, as if Margaret needed any more convincing.

"I would be glad to have you," she finally said with a smile, "but don't you have work at the station?"

Decha broke into a grin. "My shift just ended. I am not very skillful, but please let me help you." Margaret gave a nod in response, before resuming her pace.

"By the way," chirped her new companion, "what you did at the police station was incredible! So brave! Nobody has ever done that before. I don't know how you can do something like that!" Margaret shook her head in embarrassment at the reputation she had obviously gained. But Decha made it even worse when he concluded: "I think they will call you the 'white tigress' from now on!" It was no doubt meant as a compliment, but the comment only served to finalize her mortification. *Oh, what have I done?*

The unlikely duo strode back to the office with a hint of hope in their step; not the rosy kind, but the practical type that sustained the spirit. The rain had stopped, leaving in its wake a warm afternoon glow. The sunlight was a welcome sensation for Margaret, but the cheery

Thai man beside her was what warmed her the most. For all she knew, they were walking back to the pits of hell, yet she felt more prepared for it now. *Optimism,* that was the word.

Back at the office, Morris and Jeremy were speechless with surprise at Margaret's return with a stranger. Introductions were made all around, and after a quick shot of coffee, she joined the team's efforts at plotting out the captors' possible route, considering all the clues they had received. No one had any misconceptions that this would be a fruitful task, but it kept their minds occupied, and who knew, they might just be able to infer Mya's destination. It was during these twilight hours—waiting for a call, emotions taut, hands itching for something to do—that Chariya's comforting presence became invaluable; she always knew just the right words that every team member needed to hear. In a way, the waiting became a sort of oasis, a space to breathe in between spurts of grueling action.

5:45PM

They hadn't heard Mya's voice in more than two hours.

Worst case scenarios chased each other around in Morris' mind, dragging his thoughts into a wild dance. Jeremy had long ago given up pretending to work on other matters; his coping method was to pace around Morris' desk. Margaret had settled into a rigid vigil, glaring at Morris' phone as though her willpower alone could summon a call. Aat, Chariya and Decha also huddled near the phone, their shared silence punctuated by Chariya's occasional attempts at brightening the atmosphere.

To quell the bleak silence, Jeremy voiced a question that had been on everyone's mind. "Do you think her captors know what they're doing?"

The question hung in the air, unanswered. As humanitarian workers, they knew that perpetrators were molded by their upbringing and experiences, victims in their own twisted way. But that knowledge didn't help much in the face of unspeakable atrocities. As a model frontline practitioner, Margaret declined to reply, likely knowing that a textbook response would not help matters at such an emotional time. She seemed to understand perfectly well the limitations of rationality. Chariya inhaled, as if about to speak, but then apparently decided against it. The rest settled into the silence that had snaked back into the room.

Morris shook his head, sniffed, and offered his take in a somber tone, "I guess they grew up in impoverished homes, like the majority of the rural population. They see what wealth offers them on television and think to themselves, '*That's* what will bring me happiness'..." He shrugged his shoulders with a sigh, unconvinced by his own explanation. Jeremy grimaced in understanding, but could only shake his head in response. Likewise, the expressions of the others showed that they found no comfort in that conjecture.

Some questions might never be answered, and some answers would never be enough.

5:57PM

Ring ring, ring ring.

The room erupted, everyone scrambling to lean in as close as possible to the phone without suffocating Morris, laptops and notebooks at the ready, fingers twitching.

Morris knew the moment he put the receiver to his ear, however, that something had changed. "Sir...I'm so tired, my body hurts," whispered Mya. Her tiny voice shook. "I can't do this anymore..."

"Mya, don't give up," implored Morris, "Think of your family! Your pa, your ma, your brother...they're all waiting for you to go back to them!" The desperation was all too clear in his words, drawing concerned looks from the Americans who didn't know what was going on.

At the mention of her family, Mya broke down into weak sobs. "But I can't...I can't..." Morris knew then that familial love was not enough to sustain her. What then could he possibly say?

Mya continued through her tears, "Please tell my ma I'm so sorry. I love her so much. Tell my brother that I miss him. Tell my pa I'm sorry." Chariya quickly scrawled a message on Morris' notebook. 'ASK ABOUT AMBITIONS'.

"Mya, listen," began Morris, struggling to sound conversational rather than desperately beseeching, "Tell me about your dreams in life. What do you want to do when you grow up?"

Chariya clasped her hands tight in a gesture of fervent prayer that this topic would generate some hope.

The sobbing continued a few more moments, then lapsed into a tremulous silence. Morris had nothing. Finally, Mya's voice broke through the anticipation. "I want to open a business that will help my village in Yangon." Her voice gained some strength, "The adults need jobs and the children want to go to school. I want them to have a better life." Morris was elated at the spark of hope in her voice. *Come on, come on, Mya, you can do this!* Beside him, Chariya was clearly touched by the young girl's beautiful heart for her people.

"So, what will you do, Mya?" inquired Morris, "What kind of business do you want to open?" More details, more details. The more details he could elicit, the more realistic the dream, the more hope-inducing this effort would be.

"I love to draw..." replied Mya. "I think I could design clothes and other things, and then our village could make them and sell them—" Her words were cut off by loud banging on a door, and a voice telling Mya this would be her last warning. "Mr. Morris, thank you for everything you have done...but I know it's impossible –"

"No! We've almost found you, Mya!"

"Thank you...but I don't know if I can call again—"

"Mya, don't give up, just leave your phone on—" But the line had gone dead.

"No..." Eyes vacant, Morris could only stare at the phone in his hands. "No, no, no...." The air had been sucked out of the room in an instant.

Everything they had gone through in the past eight hours, everything they had tried...it couldn't all have amounted to nothing. Everyone was holding back tears. Chariya rushed out of the room, wiping at her face. Jeremy put his arm on Morris' shoulder. Words of comfort had long eluded them, leaving nothing but a bad taste in their mouths.

"She thanked me...for what...for what..." The Burmese man had sunk to unparalleled depths of despair, from which none of his coworkers could rescue him.

Eventually, the expression of disbelief etched on his face morphed into one of purpose. It was time. No more waiting, no more phone calls. It was now or never. He stood up and gathered his things without a word, and as if on cue, Aat stood up as well, car keys ready in hand. Jeremy, who had known Morris ever since he joined them as an intern, sat him back down, gently but firmly.

"Morris, listen, I know what you're thinking, but that won't work." Morris looked away, jaw tight with surging emotions. "Trust me, I wish more than anything I could go out there with you to find her, to do something other than just wait around. But..." Here he let out a massive sigh, "This is the best way we can help her, you know? If you leave, who's going to talk to Mya the next time she calls?"

His words made sense to Morris, but did nothing to quench the blazing fire in his heart.

Aat stayed standing, looking away into empty space, a husk of the sociable young man who had joined their ranks just a few hours ago.

Finally, Decha stepped in. "I know how you feel, Morris," he began, his voice tender. "There was this robbery once, where they took a civilian hostage. I wanted so badly to rush in and save her, but my commander told me to stand down."

Here his voice began to quiver at the memory, but with a brief pause, he managed to steady himself. "In the end, I had to watch as he shot her, then himself." He closed his eyes, reliving the traumatic moment. His voice sunk to a whisper: "I wanted to shoot my commander, the robbers...and then that night, at home, I wanted to shoot myself."

None of his listeners knew how to respond. What could be said in the face of such painful honesty?

Off to the side, Aat's eyes began to refocus, like an ice statue thawing back to life. There was an aura of warmth spreading throughout the entire tiny office, carried by Decha's heartfelt words.

He continued, eyes red: "I know what it's like to be forced to wait and do nothing, and the fear that waiting will cost you everything." Here, Margaret put a hand on his shoulder, Chariya's hand soon joining it. "But I've come to learn that waiting is not a weakness. If I had acted that day, who knows what would have happened? Maybe there would have been even more dead bodies. Waiting is not weakness and action is not bravery. You are so brave, and you're doing so much for Mya already, Morris." Decha ended his story with an arm around Morris' shoulder, two men united not by blood or even nationality, but by their concern for the oppressed. Their camaraderie radiated throughout the office, pushing back the cold dejection.

They all knew then that the only thing they could do—the best thing to do, as maddening as it was—was wait for the next call.

6:37PM

Despite their obvious lack of appetite, Margaret forced the team to take a dinner break, although there was a hint of compassion in her usually authoritative tone. Morris and Jeremy ate at the office pantry while she ate alone, keeping watch over Morris' phone. Decha, Aat and Chariya went downstairs to buy takeout food, hoping to spend as little time as possible outside of earshot of the phone.

On their way out, Chariya noticed Aat's atypical quietness, and the way he stared mostly at the ground. In one such moment, he looked up to find her gazing inquisitively at him and confessed, speaking in Thai, "I...don't think I should go back with you. I haven't managed to help at all, and even managed to ruin your efforts."

She took a step toward him, but he backed away. Decha stood aside, knowing that what Aat said was not totally untrue. He continued, "I'm just a driver...I don't know much about anything besides cars and roads. So, I think I'm going to go now. Tell them I'm sorry for my mistake." And before either of his friends could say anything, he walked away. Chariya sighed as Decha made off after him, then followed as quickly as she could.

"Hey, Aat! Listen," said Decha when he caught up, "the mistake you made was bad. But you're a man, so you have to take responsibility.

Don't run away—come back with us instead and do your best to make things right."

He put a hand on Aat's shoulder as he turned him back to the direction of the office. Chariya was silent, listening. "Everybody makes mistakes. You just have to learn to move on and do better next time." Aat's reluctant footsteps gradually synced with Decha's firm steps as they made their way back, a relieved Chariya in tow.

Back at the office, everyone had difficulty eating. Food never tasted so much like sand; every bite, every morsel was a chore. One could almost hear the molars grinding away at the food, mere machines fulfilling a banal task. Vacant stares mirrored empty stomachs. There was life, but just barely. Every second that passed was a lifetime away from finding Mya. How could they *enjoy* food—or anything else— knowing what Mya was going through? Ten minutes of filling—but far from satisfying—food was clearly all that Morris could handle. He put his fork down. Jeremy quickly followed suit. There seemed nothing left to say, no emotion they had not shared in the past nine hours, and so they settled into a tired silence that granted them only physical relief. The others chewed their food quietly, almost apologetically, uncertain whether talking would lighten the mood or else simply disrupt one another's rest.

7:00PM

It had been more than an hour since the last call. The unspoken fear was that Mya might not even attempt to call again, given her state of abject despondency in their last conversation.

Life in the office appeared to return to its familiar pattern, but in a wholly unfamiliar way. Each of the staff members had their own duties to complete: Margaret needed to prepare for meetings with notable politicians in the coming week; Jeremy had mountains of reports to write about the projects he oversaw; Morris was scheduled for a meeting with a local contact the next morning. Yet there were relics of their shared experience strewn around the office: the illegible notebooks; the red marker discarded by Jeremy; the webpages opened to find Central Plaza, KFC, temples, street names; the phone, resting in its receiver so peacefully, as if it did not hold the key to saving a life. Everything had been imbued with new meaning, with a piece of their bleak memory, a piece of their broken hearts.

Even as they continued with their work, their minds were fixed on Mya, a part of their peripheral consciousness perpetually fixated on Morris' phone. For any one of them to forget Mya was to commit emotional amputation. Meanwhile, the three newcomers kept faithful watch over the phone, occasionally making polite conversation to ease the dreary quietness.

The phone rang.

The team looked at each other, surprise written over their faces.

Morris quickly picked up the phone, "Hello?" Once again, they could make out ambient car noises. Mya had given them another chance to eavesdrop—perhaps their last chance to pinpoint her location. The team's jubilance was instantly replaced with this somber realization. The pressure was all too real.

"...But Siam Nights has better beds," remarked one of the captor's voices. Aat's eyes lit up as he scrawled across his notebook, 'SIAM NIGHTS HOSTEL'. The group leaned in even closer to the phone, burning with anticipation at such a significant clue as to Mya's destination. Perhaps this would be the breakthrough they so desperately needed.

"I don't care about the beds!" exclaimed the other voice, "It's too boring, there aren't any bars nearby. Let's stay at the Somjai instead. You know you miss the girl who works there." This last statement drew a chuckle from the first voice. 'SOMJAI', Aat quickly added. The conversation drifted to the finer points of the famed damsel, then to other mundane topics, bringing the hushed team's anticipation to its absolute limit. They had to do something about this new clue. Jeremy and Aat, being the most practical-minded of the group, started to sneak from their chairs, aiming for Jeremy's laptop.

CRASH!

The group fell from their seats, shaken by the sudden sound from the phone. Confused glances were exchanged—what had happened? Margaret was the first to recover, mouthing the words "car crash" as the group nodded in agreement, all eyes wide with dread.

"Stupid motorcycle!" raged the driver's voice. There came the sound of a door opening, followed by a distant argument between him and another voice— presumably the motorcyclist. After a few minutes of heated exchange, the kidnapper's voice suddenly took on an urgent, pleading tone.

Chariya quickly typed on her laptop, "He's telling the man not to call the police." The atmosphere in the office instantly became thick with tangible apprehension. They didn't know whether to be glad or dismayed that the accident wasn't more serious.

Jeremy and Margaret were muttering under their breath, "Come on, come on, come on!", willing the motorcyclist to call the police. Decha had his phone in his hands, ready to call his friends at the station to find out the location of the traffic accident. They became even more riveted as the van driver's voice became increasingly frantic, then angry, yelling at the motorcyclist in the hopes of scaring him away.

It was at this moment that the team heard Mya begin speaking, crying out weakly, "Save me, save me." As she recovered from the crash, her voice quickly grew louder and louder—and was suddenly muffled, likely by the hand of the remaining kidnapper. Chariya covered her own mouth in shock, tears in her eyes as she listened to whatever obscene threats were being whispered into Mya's ears.

They listened with dismay to the choking start of the motorcycle engine, then the receding noise as it rattled away...along with their fervent hope for salvation. The van roared as the captor gunned the engine, masking Mya's sobs. Morris buried his face in his hands, unable to cope with what had just happened. The same sense of incredulity and horror engulfed the others, trapping them in a limbo wherein nobody could express their grief aloud for fear of the phone, and nobody could leave the room for fear of missing out.

Decha managed to recover first, remembering to text his friend at the police station, telling him to keep his ears open in case the motorcyclist reported the accident. Then he hugged his knees in a seated fetal position, as if to protect himself from the situation so similar to his past.

Margaret made her way out of the office as quietly as humanly possible to call the police superintendent with the location update. But as she would tell the others later, all she got in response was the tired explanation that they could not do anything without more concrete leads; in this case, when the van might stop at the mentioned hostels. With the unexpected accident, there really was no telling how long it would take them to arrive, assuming they did at all.

She hung up, a thousand reasons swirling in her mind to just go and set up watch at the hostels themselves, along with a thousand counterarguments why this would not be the best course of action. In all her years of work, she had always preferred a visible enemy over internal conflict; the former mostly resulted in victory with some inevitable bruises, the latter yielded defeat with nothing but a migraine to show for it.

Time for an aspirin or three.

7:20PM

Twenty minutes later, the line was still alive, filling the office with more ambient car noise. No more useful information had surfaced. The kidnappers were probably drained from driving all day, so conversation had waned.

The intermittent sound of Mya's muffled crying continued, simultaneously breaking their hearts and keeping their emotions burning, each sob chipping away at them bit by painful bit. Bathroom breaks no longer signified a biological need; they provided a space to breathe, to move, to make a sound, to waken the senses again, even if it was only water flowing from a rusty faucet.

With their auditory senses deadened from the prolonged silence, their eyes finally registered the darkness that had descended on the office. The sun had set long ago, but nobody had noticed during all the action and agitation. The gloom mirrored and refracted their dejection, as if their physical senses needed to be reminded of their inner turmoil. Only the lights in the pantry were on, and nobody had the motivation to brighten the room. For what? Some things were better left muffled in the shadows.

And so six somber statues sat around the desk with a single phone, broadcasting forlorn noises.

To the ignorant observer, it might have resembled some strange ritual of serenity. The phone their idol, the desk their altar, the chairs their pews. Praying for peace, waiting for it with all of their energy. To the six, every object and person constituted a deplorable sacrament, one that purged them of all hope and baptized them in ineffable destitution. Not a sound was to be heard from them but the occasional sniffle or cough. Not a sight was to be seen, but the phone on speaker mode, resting on the desk.

Morris, who had long ago finished preparations for his meeting the next day, stared at the phone, head in his hands. He peered through a crack between his fingers, in the hopes of gaining some new perspective. None came, and so he glanced at the others.

Jeremy's eyes were fixated on the phone, twiddling his thumbs. He had seemingly convinced himself that he needed yet another coffee break—one that never quite made it back to work. Besides, caffeine had ceased to induce any effect on any one of their oversaturated systems.

Back at her desk, Margaret stared at photos of herself with famous politicians and philanthropists, perhaps questioning her career. Morris could guess at what she was thinking. With every meeting she had to prepare for, she had become more disillusioned, just as they all had. If she could not even rescue a single girl from human trafficking, what good was she to the cause? Did she deserve to be a coordinator? Her network, her influence...they must now seem so far away, Morris surmised, an illusion of power that had been obliterated in the dark reality of the day's events.

The Thai helpers sat quietly, exhibiting more of a calm composure than their American counterparts. However, they did not have the luxury of peripheral tasks as a distraction; their imaginations were likely running wild, none of their thoughts positive ones. Tonight, suffering was a chameleon, shifting shapes and colors to crush every unwilling participant. From this beast there was no hiding, and frankly, Morris knew that none of them were bothering to try anymore.

And so the six sat, silent in the empty office—waiting for clues, waiting for a miracle.

Waiting to see if the darkness could grow any darker.

7:30PM

"Finally!" declared the driver's voice, piercing the darkness like a flash of lightning. Morris and Margaret snapped to attention, and she quickly joined the circle of listeners. Jeremy and Aat took longer to awaken from their semi-slumber, stretching their stiff necks. Chariya quickly rubbed the grogginess from her eyes.

"And we would've arrived earlier if not for that stupid motorcyclist," the other captor responded, voice brimming with impatience. Decha glanced at his watch and noted down the time, ready to also write down which hostel the young men had finally decided on.

"Do you see the girl?" teased the driver. "I think I see her! And she's looking at you, she's winking at you. Oh, you have a girlfriend now!" He burst into laughter, while his companion only offered feeble comebacks.

The girl, the girl...that meant the Somjai!

Decha had clearly come to the same conclusion. He dashed outside to call the station, with Margaret hot on his heels. She probably hadn't known what the driver said, but any police-related clue could potentially benefit from her influence.

"...Why are there so many cars?" cried the exasperated driver. "Where am I supposed to park?"

The other voice tried to soothe him, "Don't get angry. Let's just wait here a bit, someone will probably leave soon."

But the agitated driver would have none of it. "Who the hell leaves a hostel in the middle of the night? People come here to *sleep!*"

"Okay okay okay!" offered the other voice, heavy with exasperation. "Let's just go to Siam then! Calm down, man." The car returned to its familiar kinetic quietness, but brains were cranking in full gear at the office—this latest development meant that Decha was now relaying outdated information.

Before anyone could stop him, Aat darted toward the office door to Margaret and Decha, knocking a chair over in his haste. Everyone's eyes widened in stupefaction. A split second later, Chariya's hand flew to the phone, trying to cover the microphone.

Too late.

"What was that?" the driver's voice rang out from the office phone. "Did you hear that?"

"Yeah, it came from the back," came the reply. "Hey...hey, *hey* girl! What have you got—"

The phone disconnected.

8:25PM

What have you got.
What have you got.
What have you got.
It had been an hour since the disconnection, yet the incomplete sentence echoed in the air, stuck on repeat. Sounds no longer mattered; the silence roared ceaselessly.

The police had finally sent out patrol cars to the Siam Nights hostel, but a thirty-minute wait turned up nothing. Margaret and Decha—with her influence and his contacts—could only barely persuade them to check out the Somjai as well, with the same result and the same disappointment. What little progress they had made so far was ground to a screeching halt. Numb was the new catchword.

What have you got.
What have you got.
What have you got.

8:50PM

Two mistakes in a single day. That was it for Aat, the simple driver who grew up on a humble farm. He had never asked for this mission, nor had he known what it would entail when he agreed to sign on. This only made the guilt worse—he had no idea how to handle such immense consequences.

And so he ran, and nobody stopped him.

He ran out of the office. Ran down the stairs. Ran to his motorcycle. He drove mindlessly, aimlessly through the streets, the lights and noises flying by in a blur. All he knew was that he needed to get away.

Somehow, he finally found himself parked in front of the Siam Nights hostel. Even as his vision became blurred with tears, even as he shook his head, a force—some gut feeling—drove him to walk into the hostel and ask the staff if they had noticed a car with a dent on it. It was not a course of action that he expected to lead to a positive outcome; no, it was simply Decha's voice in his mind, telling him that he must do his best to make things right.

He was stunned speechless when the girl at the counter said that yes, there was in fact a dented car parked right outside. Aat gaped, then dashed outside without another word. He didn't see a white van. He sprinted to the first row of cars parked along the road. Still nothing. He raced through the parking lot. No white van there either. *Where was it?!* Baffled and out of breath, he ran back to the counter and yelled at the receptionist. "*Where is the van?*"

The terrified girl retreated to the wall with a stuttered reply. "Wh- what white van?"

"You said there was a dented white van parked outside! You said you saw it!"

Her eyes widened, her head shaking vehemently, "I-I-I didn't say I saw a white van! I saw a *car* with a dent in it! It's a gray car! Not a van!"

Once again, Aat could not believe what he was hearing.

What have you got.

Mutely, without a hint of anger, he turned around and stumbled back outside. That was it, then. He sat on his motorcycle, folded his arms over the handlebars, and buried his face in the nook. Here was the one spot left in the world, it seemed, without failures, without condemnation, without guilt.

What have you got.

9:45PM

They sat, silent in the empty office, their minds, if it was possible, even more numb than before, the silence louder than ever.

It had become hard to differentiate between noise, silence, and pure imagination. The only colors were shades of black, shadows within shadows. The stagnant air was inhaled, exhaled, then breathed back in again. The occasional sniffs remained, but it seemed even Chariya had long ago cried herself bone dry. All that remained now was the wait.

To the original office trio—Morris, Jeremy, and Margaret—waiting felt like all they had ever done, and all they would ever do. They could hardly remember what life was like before Mya's call. It was as short as a phone call away, yet distant as a lifetime.

11:00PM

A father and son were walking along the beach, where tens of thousands of starfish were stranded on the sand, washed up by a storm. There they lay, like so many bone fragments of the sea.

Every couple of steps the father would bend over, pick up a starfish, and throw it as far as he could back into the sea. The son watched silently until he couldn't contain his curiosity any longer, "Dad, why do you do that? You know you can't save all these starfish!"

The father replied with a glimmer in his eyes, "If I don't throw them back into the sea, they will all die when the sun gets high."

Still perplexed, the son prodded, "But there are so many starfish here! You can't make much difference by saving only one at a time."

Smiling at his son's persistence, the father bent over, picking up yet another starfish. He paused, weighed it in his hand, then threw it far, far away, back into the sea.

"It made all the difference to that one."

Morris jolted awake from his accidental slumber.

"Hey, there," Jeremy greeted him, offering a steaming mug of coffee. "Didn't want to wake you up—God knows we all need a bit of rest today."

Morris downed the coffee, somewhat energized from his brief rest. Chariya stirred and also woke from her nap, eyes bloodshot from a restless sleep. Decha, true to his profession, had apparently remained vigilant, asking his colleagues for any case files on forced prostitution or kidnappings within the proximity of the two hostels. Yet even with all his energy and zeal, he informed them morosely that he'd managed to get nowhere, running into wall after immovable wall.

Margaret walked over, her work materials packed away. "I'm going to call it a day; I have a busy day tomorrow. I recommend you all do the same." They turned to her, checking the time, yawning and returning to a destitute reality.

Her face said she loathed to be the first one to leave despite her words. Still, they all knew that life outside the office must go on, and that Margaret had a host of other obligations. She gave them each a firm squeeze on the shoulder. Her hand lingered a moment on Decha. "You've proven yourself today. It's time to let go of our failures and take pride in the fact that we never gave up."

Margaret was halfway out of the office when she suddenly stopped, turned around, and said with a sheepish smile, "Good job today, all of you. I couldn't have asked for a better team." And with that, she closed the door on the day, along with its tears, frustrations, and heartbreak.

The remaining quintet eventually decided that there would be no more calls that night. As difficult as the decision was, Morris knew he could not wait indefinitely for Mya. It was time for him to let go too.

And so they packed up their day, each item, each belonging weighed down with emotions. Jeremy closed the map on his laptop, hurriedly scrubbing his face as he did so. Most of the others stepped out of the office without a word. Only Chariya had the strength left to offer whispered words of encouragement—words that, to Morris, sounded empty given the outcome. As the lights were switched off, a visual veil of black silence was cast over the office—their own microcosm of human frailty imploding into darkness.

March 10th
12:03AM

"Daddy's home!"

"Daddy!"

Jeremy could never understand how his children—Daniel, eight, and Anong, six—had such endless energy, tonight least of all. It felt like someone had beaten him to a pulp. Every joint was aching, every limb sore. There was always a certain guilt associated with coming home late or leaving shortly right after returning home on some spontaneous operation, but tonight, turmoil drowned the guilt.

"What're you two naughty cupcakes doing up this late?" he said, smiling at their contagious enthusiasm.

Here they were, his beloved jewels, squealing and jumping and complaining about each other, with nothing but the smallest cares in the world to worry about, just as it should be. Jeremy had never been happier to hear Anong vent animatedly about Daniel stealing her teddy bear to reenact the scene from "The Revenant"—the father and son's favorite movie—and Daniel interrupting his sister to get his version of the story in. They spoke mostly in English, but threw in the occasional insult to each other in Thai, thinking he wouldn't understand.

Jeremy swept them up in his arms, only

wishing he could hold them like this forever, protecting them forever against the world lurking at their threshold. "Daddy loves you, you know that, right?"

Little Anong studied her father's arm curiously. "Daddy, why is your arm red?" Jeremy looked down at the smeared remains of the word 'CAR', repeated over his forearm, and was rendered speechless.

"Does it say... 'car', Daddy?" asked his son. "Can we draw on your hands too?"

Jeremy's eyes began to sting, and he had to look away from his expectant children. "No, not tonight, Daniel."

He looked up at Boonsri, quietly glowing, dutifully carrying out a tray laden with his dinner. "Alright, you two muffins," he said to the children. "Time to go to bed. I don't even know what you're doing still up. You're tired, aren't you, Anny? Come here, give me a kiss first. Off you go now." His gaze followed them as they jostled each other to their shared room. God knew he loved them equally, but tonight he couldn't help looking more at his daughter. An image flashed across his eyes, the inside of a van, and he blinked hard to breathe again.

Boonsri set the table as he sat down. He wasn't hungry, but yearned for some semblance of normalcy. "Thanks, honey." Jeremy's mother had always wanted him to marry a nice Southern girl, but when he introduced her to Boonsri, beautiful, gentle, and able to cook absolutely anything into a heavenly meal, his mother began asking him when they would get married. That had been ten years ago now, and his love for his wife and her motherland had only grown since then, despite the atrocities he witnessed on the job.

"You look tired, how are you?" asked Boonsri, giving her husband a massage. Her fingers always managed to find his sorest spots.

"I'm..." He caught his breath, but didn't try again, settling for a hand over his wife's hand, bringing her around into his arms with a sigh. The cutlery clattered to the table. Neither of them had to say a word as he leaned into her.

"Can you...remind me again, Boon?" He closed his eyes, willing himself to remember her words.

"Yes, of course," she smiled. "Jeremy Moore, you chose this work because of love, not because you wanted to be the hero. You didn't want money or fame. You love me, you love your children, you love Thailand and you love my people. This country is not for you or any one person to save. But you are still *our* hero, always." She gave him a peck on the forehead, a gentle squeeze, and began to clear the table.

"Thanks, honey. And hey, sorry I didn't text you at lunch..." With another understanding smile, Boonsri left to tuck their children into bed.

Somehow, his wife, his children, always managed to calm the bad days—days where his brain would refuse to stop whirring and spinning like a broken movie projector, screaming out the day's failures for an audience of one. Here at home, Jeremy was reminded of his place in the world, and the world's place in him.

He opened his laptop and began to look online for GPS trackers. Only when he found the perfect one did he allow himself to go to bed, his wife long asleep. He had ordered two.

***

In his dream, Morris saw himself, two years younger, talking with Margaret. She had been prepping him on the duties of the role he was applying for.

"Okay, Morris, last question," said Margaret. Morris wiped his palm surreptitiously on his pants, taking a deep breath. "Why do you want to do this work?"

The perfect question—he had prepped for it weeks in advance. "I would like to enter this career because—"

But his interviewer shook her head. "No, *why* do you want to do this work? Not this job, not this NGO—this line of work."

"I..." Morris didn't know. It was that simple. No matter how he stuttered, paused, desperately thought, he couldn't come up with a satisfying answer. "It's...meaningful...challenging. No, rewarding. No. I'm sorry, Ms. Margaret, I don't know." Margaret nodded slightly, signifying the end of the interview, and he reluctantly stood up to leave.

"I guess I want to help people," he tried one last time.

"But there are many ways to help, and many people who need help."

"You're right." He stopped at the door, turned and said, "Please, Ms. Margaret, I hope that you'll consider me. I don't know what else I can do."

"Can?" She raised a questioning eyebrow. "With your CV, Morris, I believe you can do whatever you want in a number of enviable positions. Career advancement should not be a concern."

"I..." He gulped. "What I mean is, I can't settle for any other job. I just can't do it. My heart won't let me."

"What do you mean?"

"I might be able to succeed in another field, but I want to succeed *here*. In the fight against human trafficking."

Margaret leaned forward in her chair. "Morris, think on this. What do you mean your heart won't let you?"

"I need to make it stop—stop the bad guys from destroying Thailand's children..."

The dream was burning at the edges, flickering, blurring. "Morris, what if you never win the fight? What if there is no victory, ever?"

"I will prove myself to you, Ms. Margaret, I promise. Please reconsider..." The dreaming Morris wanted to wake up, just wake up, from this dream that had contorted, tearing suddenly at his heartstrings.

"What if you never win the fight?" Margaret was looming larger, bigger than life, filling the room. "Morris, *why are you here?*"

Then complete darkness, in the blink of an eye. Morris was awake, in his own bed, blankets tangled, beads of sweat on his forehead. The question rang in his ears, echoing in the stillness. A car honked outside in the street below.

"Because...because my heart is here..." he whispered into the darkness, as tears dripped onto the pillow.

March 10th, 2010
9:15AM

For the first time in his entire life, Morris had not felt like going to work.

He felt emotionally hungover, his head swollen and throbbing with the previous day's concoction of expired feelings, his thoughts sluggish, yet still jumpy from his nightmare. He felt just as tired waking up as he had been falling asleep.

Returning to the office, Morris shared a sad smile with Jeremy and Margaret, the dark circles beneath their own eyes making it painfully evident that they had all enjoyed a near-sleepless night.

But here he was, at his desk back at the office. Here they all were, choosing to return to this place of untold trials and ordeals. Change was in the air, but nobody could ascertain what kind. Jeremy and Margaret peered at Morris behind his back, no doubt wondering if he had the strength to carry on. Some crises kill you, not with their impact, but with the aftermath.

The phone rang, startling them.

Ring ring, ring ring, ring ring.

They exchanged looks. Morris knew it wouldn't be Mya. He knew he would be disappointed. He knew that this phone, this job, this life would never be the same again.

But that didn't matter. Not to whoever was on the other end of the line.

With a deep breath, he picked up the phone.

"Hello, this is Morris of the help hotline. How can I help you?"

June 2nd, 2016
7:30PM

Margaret stood on stage, eyes roaming the packed audience in front of her. Their applause was deafening—a sign of their hearty approval of her winning the International Humanitarian Award for her work in Thailand. She cleared her throat, gave a hard look at the script in her hands—and then stuffed it in her pocket.

"Six years ago, I would have been proud of myself for standing on stage like this, accepting this prestigious award. I would have savored the applause, the limelight. But six years ago, I met Mya—or should I say, *didn't* meet her. She was a girl who called our help hotline, telling us that she had been kidnapped. A series of phone calls and much painful waiting ensued, lasting the entire day. We never managed to find her, and to this day, we have no idea what became of her.

"People are often asking me, 'Marg, how do you move on from your setbacks?' And Mya would always come to mind. I can honestly tell you that I think of her every single day. Some might say I never moved on after her, but I disagree. For me, moving on doesn't mean forgetting. Indeed, if I ever do forget Mya, I would question my own humanity. No, for me, moving on means holding on to hope. I was never one to hope, until I saw firsthand the power of hope in my coworkers, Morris and Jeremy, and in a few brave Thai locals."

She paused, swallowing down still-painful emotions that conjured up memories of how her colleagues had given their absolute all on that fateful day. In her mind's eye she saw the bathroom stall door, the red marker, the fallen chair.

Taking a deep breath, Margaret continued: "Moving on for me is about honoring Mya every day with my work. And so I do not feel that this award should draw attention to me. Instead, I give it to the Morrises and Jeremys of humanitarian work, the nameless sea of men and women on the front line who somehow find the strength to move on every single day. I give it to the local practitioners who have stepped far outside their comfort zones to confront the evil in their own land."

She blinked hard, but did not falter.

"And last but certainly not least, I give it to the Myas of the world, the boys and girls who disappear into the darkness without anyone knowing or caring. Every one of you sitting here has chosen a life that requires you to face great evil, and to move on from it. Never give up, because Mya is still out there, and a thousand more just like her. Thank you."

The story continues in
*Book 2: **"When Hope Fights"***
Available now on Amazon

Epilogue

This book is based on a true story, one taken from the pages of Matthew Friedman's book "Where Were You?". The ending is true: the young girl never called again, and they never found out what happened to her. I would say, "Such is life," but I refuse to. Life should not have such stories to tell. Young girls do not belong on vans, kidnapped or deceived to be sold like objects. I tell this story because I hate its ending.

I hope you hate the ending too.

Mya was never found. But the darker reality is, there are currently 45.8 *million* girls, boys, women, and men just like her, taken from their homes and loved ones to become slaves. Many work without pay. Many suffer physical and emotional torture. Many die without ever seeing their families again. And these atrocities are taking place in every single country on the planet, not only in developing countries like Cambodia and Vietnam, but also in America and European countries.

This is *not* a solitary story—it is a story of those 45,800,000 modern slaves.

And this story is a small testament to the thousands of front-line human rights workers who dedicate their lives to combat this global atrocity; for them, this is not fiction, but a daily reality. They are unsung heroes who face more funerals than victory parades. But they march on because they hate the story's ending with a passion.

What if I told you that YOU can change the story's ending?

The truth is, if everyone cared, Mya's story would never take place. If everyone kept an eye out for the signs of human trafficking and slavery, modern slavery would be greatly reduced.

So, what can you do?

Go on Google, search for "human trafficking", and read the top three articles. Then share them with your closest friends. Believe it or not, those two actions have already changed the world for the better. If you want to do even more, go find a local NGO that addresses the issue. If there are no local ones, start an event with a friend or two; make a short film about slavery, host a movie/documentary screening ("Nefarious" is the one that gets me crying every time I watch it), invite a guest speaker to your school/company (Matthew Friedman is highly recommended), do a slavery-themed music show or art exhibit, or anything that utilizes the talents that you have. The first three steps you can take are simple, just go to www.davidsmlui.com.

Another thing you can do is write a short review of this book on Amazon or Goodreads, as this spreads the word online, reaching more people who do not know about the plight of human trafficking victims. Here is the link: https://www.amazon.com/dp/B074KL8LH5

Goodreads:

https://www.goodreads.com/book/show/36043
721-when-hope-calls?from_search=true

And of course, tell your friends and family about this book, and human trafficking. Just say, "Did you know...?" or "Check this book out..." Don't forget to check out Book 2: "When Hope Fights", as well! https://www.amazon.com/dp/B08DXJHS 2Q

The one thing I want you to know is this: You can stop human trafficking *if you put your heart to it*. Despite its ending, the story of Mya stands not for human weakness, but for hope. **Now go and do something about it.**

About the Author

David Lui is a counselor and writer based in Hong Kong, dedicated to fighting modern slavery and human trafficking. You can keep up to date with his latest books and more by signing up for David's newsletter at www.davidluiwriter.wordpress.com.

You can find him on Facebook as well.

Made in the USA
Monee, IL
04 January 2021